# Death Wind

# Death Wind

## William Bell

orca soundings

ORCA BOOK PUBLISHERS

**Librar**y and Archives Canada Cataloguing in Publication
Bell, William, 1945-
Death wind
ISBN 978-1-55143-543-5 (bound) / ISBN 978-1-55143-215-1 (pbk.)
I.Title. PS8553.E4568D42 2002     jC813'.54     C2002-910138-7
PZ7.B41187De 2002

**Summary:** When Allie fears she is pregnant, she leaves home with
Razz, a skateboard champion. Returning home she is caught up in
a tornado that threatens to destroy everything. She learns to
believe in herself and face her future.

First published in the United States, 2002
**Library of Congress Control Number:** 2002101408

Orca Book Publishers gratefully acknowledges the support for
its publishing programs provided by the following agencies: the
Government of Canada through the Book Publishing Industry
Development Program and the Canada Council for the Arts, and the
Province of British Columbia through the BC Arts Council and
the Book Publishing Tax Credit.

Cover design by Teresa Bubela
Cover photography by Eyewire

ORCA BOOK PUBLISHERS
PO Box 5626, STN. B
VICTORIA, BC CANADA
V8R 6S4

ORCA BOOK PUBLISHERS
PO Box 468
CUSTER, WA USA
98240-0468

www.orcabook.com
Printed and bound in Canada.
Printed on 100% PCW recycled paper.
12  11  10  09  •  9  8  7  6

*Dedicated to those who suffered through the*
*Barrie Tornado, and to those who helped.*
—W.B.

# Chapter One

Allie's parents were arguing again.

Allie slammed her bedroom door, rolled onto her bed and stared at the ceiling. *Eight o'clock in the morning and they're at it already*, she thought. She tried to block out the noise, but the harsh words made their way upstairs and through her door. Her mother was a shrieker. The madder she got, the higher her voice went. Her father was a rumbler. When he got mad, his voice got deeper—and he would have the Hurt Look on his face.

They were arguing about Allie again. It was the old story. Her mother said her father was "too soft" and let Allie get away with too much. After she shrieked for awhile, Allie's father would say her mother was "too stiff" and she should give a little. *Right on*, thought Allie as she lay on her bed. *I wonder what you guys would think if you knew the mess that I'm in now.*

Allie climbed out of her bed and plunked herself down in the chair at her little desk, leaning on her elbows and cupping her hands over her ears. *Stop!* She cried, inside her head. *Stop arguing!*

The report card lying on the messy desktop caught her eye. She groaned, flipping the stiff yellow booklet open. There were three bright red circles on it.

She had failed three out of four subjects. Last year she had stood near the top of her class, but this year, since she started going out with Jack, her marks had dropped. Her nickname used to be "Brainy"—Razz had given it to her in grade seven—but no one was using it lately.

Allie looked across the room to the calendar. There was a big photo of a pink kitten batting a ball of blue yarn with its tiny paw. The yarn was all tangled around the kitten's legs and head. Below the photo the days of the month were arranged in neat rows. May 1 had a red circle around it, drawn in crayon. Today was May 6.

Allie was five days overdue. She was afraid she was pregnant. *Wouldn't that be just my luck*, she thought. Jack had dumped her three weeks ago. He had told her in the cafeteria at lunchtime, while stuffing fries and gravy into his mouth. He told her he didn't want to be pinned down anymore. But they could still be friends, he had said. *Yeah, sure,* thought Allie, *you'll be my buddy if I'm knocked up, won't you, Jack?*

Allie wondered now what she had ever seen in Jack. He was cute, sure, and a lot of fun. And it had made Allie feel good when she stole Jack from that snob, Angela Burrows. But for the last couple of months he hadn't paid much attention to her. Except for sex. Allie knew she could never tell him about the red circle on her calendar.

The shrieking and rumbling downstairs got louder. Her parents were arguing about money now. Allie looked down at the three red circles on the report card, then back at the red circle on the calendar. She could imagine what would happen when her parents found out. Her father would put on the Hurt Look and make her feel super guilty. Her mother would put on the I Told You So Look and start to wind up the shriek machine.

Worst of all, Allie admitted to herself, they would be right.

Allie wished she could disappear. She wanted to be like that soft white fluff on a dandelion and float away on the wind. Somewhere, anywhere but here.

Then Allie made up her mind. Maybe she *could* disappear—get away from her parents' arguing and from the four red circles.

She went to the dresser and got a scrap of paper out of her purse. She stepped outside her room to the upstairs phone and punched in the numbers on the piece of paper. Allie cupped her hand around the mouthpiece of the phone.

"Hello."

"Hello," said Allie. "Is that you, Razz?"

"You're talkin' to him."

"This is Allie," she said. *Will he remember?* she thought. *I hope so, or I'll look like a total goof.*

"Hey, Brainy! How are ya?"

"Okay, I guess."

Allie took a breath. *Say it,* she said to herself. "Umm, I was wondering if your offer still stands."

"Well, sure, Brainy, but I thought—"

"Things have changed," she cut in. "I'd like to go with you now. When are you leaving?"

"In about two hours. Can you be ready?"

"No probs," she answered.

"Okay, where?"

"Umm, park around the corner. Ten o'clock, right?"

"See you then, Brainy." He hung up.

Razz and Allie had been friends since forever. He lived on a farm outside of town now, but he went to the same school as Allie. Last week, she had been complaining to him about how her life was falling apart. Razz had been really concerned about her. He had even offered to take her on tour with him. The skateboarding season was starting, and Razz was leaving today.

From downstairs, Allie heard some more shrieking and rumbling. Then the kitchen door slammed. As she went back into her room and closed the door, she heard the Chevy roar to life in the driveway. She knew her mother was taking off in a fit again. She always raced the engine like that when she was throwing a fit.

Allie got her little suitcase out of the closet. It was pretty banged up—the result of a few summers at camp. Soon, the bag was packed. She sat on it so she could close the snaps. Then she got her backpack and threw in her hair dryer, brushes, combs, can of mousse, toothbrush, and makeup. Next came the Walkman and a dozen tapes, along with a couple of movie mags. Finally, she stuffed in a new box of maxi-pads.

*Here's hoping*, she said to herself. When she was packed, Allie went to her desk and ripped the report card into shreds. She dropped the pieces into the waste can. *Only one red circle left*, she thought.

Then she put a tape in the deck, turned it up high and settled down at her window to wait.

Just before ten o'clock, Allie yanked at the window. It creaked and groaned as it slid up. She dropped the suitcase and the pack out first. Then she climbed out and dropped to the flat garage roof. Allie looked around. She tossed her stuff into the backyard and slid down the drainpipe, scraping her hands.

Allie slipped between the garage and the hedge and was soon headed down the street. Before she turned the corner, she looked back at the house. The bright morning sun blazed in the windows. Her dad would be in the kitchen, working. He'd be going over the accounts, shaking his head and worrying. Behind the house, the big maple swayed in the wind. That tree was the only thing she liked about the house.

When her mom got home, Allie wouldn't be there. They would find only the note she had pinned to her pillow:

*Dear Mom and Dad,*
*I'm going away. You'll be better off without me.*
*Love, Allie.*

# Chapter Two

The first thing Allie noticed when she climbed into the van was the mattress in the back.

"Hey, wait a minute," she said.

Razz was dressed wildly, as usual. Green running shoes, unlaced. Yellow pants and a cherry red shirt. A green painter's hat.

All of her friends thought Razz was cute. He was seventeen, tall and dark.

Allie thought so too, but she had known him too long to be interested in him that way. *Besides*, she thought, *I have enough of that kind of trouble as it is.*

"Relax, Brainy," he laughed. "I'm not putting the move on ya. Take it easy."

He started the van and pulled away from the curb. Looking around, Allie's eye was caught by the skateboards. There was a rack along each side of the van and at least eight boards hung from them. They were all different colors, with wild graphics on them. The decks were different shapes, but each one had the name *RAZZ* in big letters on it. Behind her seat was a big wooden box with dozens of stickers showing company logos plastered on the lid. Behind the driver's seat was a blue SkyGrabber BMX cycle. Razz had been a BMX racer in grade nine, but now he spent all his time on a skateboard.

"Better buckle up, Brainy," Razz told her.

Allie turned around and snapped the seat belt on. "New van?" she asked."Just picked it up last week," he answered. "Like it?"

Allie checked the interior. The red carpet felt soft under her feet. The seats were covered with real sheepskin throws. There seemed to be a thousand dials and gauges on the dash. Music thumped from a tape deck that was covered with buttons.

"What kind of music is *that*?" she asked, wrinkling her nose.

"Skunk music."

"Huh?"

"Skunk—you know, skateboard punk. Like it? No? Well, there's some other stuff in the rack."

She flipped open the box on the console between the seats and got a Killjoy tape. She put it into the deck.

"Hungry?" asked Razz. He pointed to a giant jar of peanut butter and a bag of red twisters on the dashboard. "They taste great together."

"No, thanks," said Allie, trying not to screw up her face at the thought of the taste. She settled back in the soft bucket seat.

They were turning onto Highway 400. The van picked up speed. Allie kicked off her shoes and put her feet up on the dash. She watched the scenery flash past, wondering how long it would be before her parents noticed she was gone. Would they phone the cops?

Hours later they were on the outskirts of Ottawa. They stopped at a restaurant to eat. Razz had a big plate of fries with hot dog relish and ketchup on them. The green and red mess on his plate looked like one of those dumb modern paintings

Allie's art teacher raved about. Allie ordered a hamburger but couldn't eat it. When they were finished, Razz pulled a wad of money from his pocket—all twenties. He peeled a bill from the wad and handed it to Allie.

"How about you pay and I'll bring the van out front?"

"Okay, but I can pay for my own," she said.

"You can pay next time, Brainy, okay?"

When they got to the fairground, it was packed with cars, vans and people. Razz showed a pass to the cop at the gate and they drove under a huge white banner that read "Ontario Skateboard Championships." They parked on the grassy infield and got out.

"I gotta spend the afternoon prac-ticing," said Razz. "You can do what you want. But do me a favor and keep an eye on the van, okay? Last year, Slammer— he's my biggest opposition—sent a few of his goons to wreck my boards."

"Okay," said Allie. "I'll just look around. I'll watch the van."

Allie didn't know much about skateboarding, but she knew Razz was last year's national champion. He made a lot of money from sponsors. That's why you could buy boards all over North America with his name on them. This meet was the first one for the season. He was touring the whole country, and if he held onto his championship, the sponsors would keep paying. They paid enough to make Razz the richest seventeen-year-old she'd ever heard of.

Razz unlocked the back doors of the van and hopped inside to change into his gear. Allie looked at the painting on the bright silver panels of the van. It showed Razz doing a hand plant and grabbing a lot of air. He had a big smile on his face. She knew the same picture was painted on the other side of the van.

When Razz hopped out, he was wearing red tights, yellow jammers and pink shoes. He had a white helmet on and pads protected his knees and elbows. On his sky-blue T-shirt it said *Skate Tough or Go Home*. In his hand was a green board with *RAZZ* written in blue stars.

Three guys came up to them. They were all decked out in skateboarding gear. And they were all holding *RAZZ* boards.

"Hey, Razz. Just get here?" the tallest one said.

"Yup."

"Slammer's lookin' for ya," said another of the guys, smiling.

"Yeah, well, tell him I'm not home."

Razz walked away, saying over his shoulder, "Lock up for me, will ya Brainy?"

An hour or so later, Allie was sitting on the grass beside the van, soaking up the spring sunshine. She had her eyes closed.

"Well, well, well. Looks like Razz has a new chick."

Allie opened her eyes. Standing in front of her was a tall, well-built guy with pure white hair with a black streak up the middle. He was wearing skateboarding gear, but everything was black. On his T-shirt was a picture of a white skull with an ugly buzzard on top. The buzzard had an eyeball in its beak. On the shirt it said *Cheer Up and Die*.

Allie said nothing.

The guy in black grinned at her, showing his yellow, mossy teeth. "You guarding the new van?" he sneered.

Allie looked away.

The guy took a knife from his pocket and slowly opened it. He looked around. Allie's heart started to pound. He walked to the front of the van and pressed the point against the new silver paint.

"Wanna come and stay with *me* tonight, Sweetie? I can show you a better time than that loser."

"Why don't you fade away, man?" she answered, trying to keep her voice even.

The guy's grin disappeared. He began to walk along the side of the van, dragging the knife. It screeched on the metal as he went.

"Hey, you creep!" Allie shouted, getting to her feet.

The guy in black kept at it. She grabbed his shoulder as he passed her. He turned and brought his knee up into her stomach. Allie felt a sharp pain as she dropped to her knees, gasping.

He kept walking slowly, dragging the squealing knife along the side of the van. As he walked away, she saw in big letters across the back of his shirt, *Slammer.*

## Chapter Three

The next morning Allie woke to a pounding on the van doors.

She groaned and rolled over. The mattress in Razz's van was too comfortable. She closed her eyes again.

The pounding came again. "Hey, Brainy! Wake up!"

Allie pulled on her baggy jeans and unlocked the door. She checked her watch. Eight o'clock. Razz hopped into the van, dragging his sleeping bag in after him. He had slept outside on the ground.

"There are showers at the edge of the infield," he said. He searched inside a leather bag and pulled out his skateboarding gear. "I've gotta warm up. The Street competition starts in half an hour."

Allie found her backpack under the sleeping bag Razz had loaned her. "OK, thanks," she said.

"By the way, Brainy, did you see anyone hanging around the van yesterday? Some scumbag did a job on the paint."

She told him about Slammer, leaving out the part where he kneed her in the gut. Razz looked angry for only a second. Then, to Allie's surprise, he smiled.

"No sweat, Brainy," he said. "That scum is trying to get me hot, so I'll lose my edge today. But I won't let him.

I'll take care of him after the meet. Catch you later."

After Razz left, Allie hopped down from the van and locked it. She looked at the dull gray sky as the wind snatched at her long hair. *Wonder what Mom and Dad are doing now*, she thought. *Probably arguing about whose fault it is that I left. What would they think if they knew* why *I left?*

Allie headed toward the showers. She was looking forward to the competitions, to seeing Razz at his best. She hoped that it wouldn't rain.

By the time the Street competition was over, Allie knew that Razz was in a class by himself. There was only one skateboarder close to him and that was Slammer.

All the boarders wore wild clothes. Some, like Razz, wore classy rags in crazy colors. Some went the other way, trying to look poor as beggars. One guy came out in a wet suit! But all of them wore pads and helmets. They swerved, jumped off the low ramp and did all kinds of unbelievable tricks with goofy names like the Ollie, the Truck Grind and the Acid Drop.

Razz and Allie took a break and had a couple of sodas back at the van.

Razz was surrounded by kids who asked him a million questions and wanted him to sign their boards. He finally had to shoo them away.

Taking a smaller board from the rack in the van, he walked over to the big cement square. The Freestyle part of the meet was about to start. Allie followed him after carefully locking the van.

She couldn't believe what Razz could do. He swerved, danced, spun in circles, did handstands—all on that little board. There were no ramps in this competition—just the flat cement square. Razz made the Pogo and the Finger Flip look easy. The crowd yelled and cheered through his act so loudly that she could hardly hear the music. Allie caught sight of Slammer on the sidelines, waiting for his turn. He was scowling.

Razz won the Freestyle and Slammer came second.

After lunch, Allie got a good seat in the stands for the Half-Pipe competition. This was the most exciting part, and the most dangerous. Razz was winning the meet, but he and Slammer were close in points, so if Slammer made a really good showing on the half-pipe and if Razz messed up, Slammer could win overall.

Allie's seat was right above the rail, in the center of the half-pipe. When the skateboarders came up the side of the half-pipe and grabbed air, they'd be right in front of her.

The first few guys weren't very good. They didn't grab much air and she could see the fear in their eyes as they flew into the air in front of her. Not that she blamed them. This was scary stuff! One poor guy, dressed in a clown suit, missed the coping trying to do a hand-plant. He flipped into the air, then dropped back to the half-pipe, tumbling down the sides like a broken doll. The guy lay at the bottom, without moving. They took him away on a stretcher. Allie could see a little pool of blood where the kid had been lying.

Next came Razz. He was directly across from her on the other side of the half-pipe. The crowd was dead quiet, waiting for him. He took his time, strapping on the helmet, adjusting his pads. Then he did something amazing. He leaped into the air! At the highest point of his jump, he slapped his board under his feet and dropped like a stone onto the half-pipe. The wheels on the board began to sing. Razz crossed the bottom of the half-pipe, rolled up the wall in front of Allie and flew high into the air.

"Oooooooooo!" was the sound the crowd made. Allie looked at Razz's face as he flew past her. She could tell he saw nothing except the picture in his mind of what he was going to do next. He spun in the air and dropped past her again.

Razz did his 360 Hand-Plants, Rocket Airs and McTwists like no one else. He was smooth. But he was also daring. The crowd never stopped oooo-ing and ahhhh-ing until he was finished. He rose up the half-pipe across from Allie, flew into the air. He landed on his feet with his board in his hand. Then he smiled and bowed, holding his board across his chest so everyone could see *RAZZ* written across the graphics.

Everybody in the stands knew that Razz had the meet in the bag now.

Slammer was next. He started safely, like the other skateboarders had. He swept up the half-pipe in front of Allie, grabbed some air, turned and dropped back down. He came back. This time he looked straight at her and, as he passed, sent a big gob of spit sailing at her. It splattered onto the bench beside her.

Then Slammer turned and dropped back. The next time he came past, he was sneering again. Allie gave him the finger. A look of surprise twisted his face into hatred.

When Slammer turned in the air, his timing was off. He dropped onto the coping. With a crack like a whip, his board snapped clean in half. The crowd gasped as he fell down the half-pipe and tumbled to a heap at the bottom. The two halves of his board clattered down beside him.

After a few seconds, he struggled to his feet. He looked back up at Allie, his face dark with hate.

# Chapter Four

That night there was a dance to wind up
the skateboarding meet. It was held in a
community center nearby. Razz asked
Allie to go with him and she said yes.
*I've got nothing better to do except worry,*
she thought.

The center was packed with kids
when Allie and Razz arrived. There were
banners and posters all over the walls,

advertising skateboards and gear. At one end of the room a few kids were doing a Freestyle demonstration on a wooden platform. The music was so loud Allie thought the roof would fall in.

Allie danced with Razz a few times. He was good. She danced with a few other guys, too. But she was nervous and kept looking around for Slammer. *Maybe he'll turn up and give me a hard time*, she thought.

At about nine o'clock Razz said to her, "Brainy, I've gotta go phone my sponsor. They wanted me to tell them how I did today. I'll be right back."

Allie sat down on one of the metal chairs, sipping a Diet Pepsi, thinking about her parents. Maybe she had made up her mind too fast. Maybe she shouldn't have left home after all. What was she going to do when Razz's tour was over? She had to admit to herself that she hadn't thought things out too well.

"Did the big shot leave you all alone?" a voice asked.

She knew the voice without looking up. It was Slammer.

He was dressed in black—black leather pants and cycle jacket. The light shining on his white hair made him look like a ghost. Standing with him were two other guys.

Slammer leaned over and hissed, "I'd have won today if it wasn't for you, bitch."

Allie could smell the beer on his breath. She didn't answer, knowing that what he said was a lie. She decided to get up and walk away. Slammer roughly shoved her back into the chair.

"Get lost," she said, wishing she felt as brave as she sounded.

"For a good-lookin' chick she's got an ugly mouth on her," said Slammer. One of the guys behind him, a tall blond kid, laughed.

Allie crossed her arms over her chest and looked away.

"Come on with us," Slammer sneered, "and we'll show you how to party."

Allie was scared. She looked around, but there was no one near her. All the kids on the dance floor had their minds on other things.

Slammer reached down and grabbed her arm, squeezing hard. He pulled her to her feet. The two goons moved in and the three of them surrounded her. Someone grabbed her other arm and yanked it behind her back. She twisted and struggled. She heard her shirt rip as a jab of pain shot into her shoulder.

"Let me go, you losers!" she yelled. But the music was so loud her voice was lost. Slammer and the two goons hustled her out the back doors of the community center. Allie shot a frantic look back over her shoulder. Just as the door slammed behind her, it flew open again. It was Razz, and he looked mad.

Slammer and the other goon let go of Allie and she stepped to the side. Slammer had his knife out—the one he had used to do the job on the van. He and the other goons separated so they could come at Razz from two sides. They paid no more attention to Allie.

"Come on, scum," hissed Slammer. "Let's get it on."

"Drop the knife, hot dog," Razz said. "Let's see if you can fight without a blade in your hand."

Slammer looked around, then folded the knife and put it into his jacket pocket. He grinned.

It was dark behind the community center and there was no one around. The cold wind whipped Allie's hair in her face. All she could do was watch as Razz and Slammer took off their jackets.

They began to circle, each fighter bent over a little, looking for an opening. Slammer struck first, aiming a kick at Razz's stomach. Razz stepped back and caught Slammer's foot. He twisted it and Slammer fell to the dirt. Razz waited for him to get up again.

Allie could see the hate in Slammer's eyes. Razz looked calm, but he had the same look of concentration he showed when he was up on the half-pipe. Slammer threw a punch. Razz ducked and the punch whacked his shoulder. He stepped forward and shoved Slammer away from him.

Again, Razz stood and waited for him. Slammer looked really mean now. *He isn't looking too good in front of his friends*, Allie thought.

Fast as a snake, Slammer bent down, grabbed a handful of dirt and flung it into Razz's face. Razz threw his hands up. Slammer lunged forward, driving his head into Razz's chest. The two of them went down, grunting, and rolled in the dirt. Fists flew. Legs jerked and kicked. Finally Razz broke loose and got to his feet, blood trickling from his nose. He wiped it away and waited for Slammer to get up.

When Slammer was on his feet, panting, Razz stepped into him and punched him just below the ribs. Allie could hear the air *whoosh* out of Slammer's lungs. With a loud grunt, Slammer dropped to his knees.

"Want some help, Slammer?" said the blond goon. *He doesn't sound too hot on the idea*, thought Allie.

"No, man. Stay out of it," Slammer wheezed.

Razz said, very calmly, "Had enough?"

"Yeah."

"Then you and your friends leave Brainy alone, all right."

Slammer looked up at her and pasted on a weak smile. "Yeah, all right."

"Okay, suppose you guys split."

The goons left, two of them helping Slammer. He wasn't walking too straight.

Later, Allie and Razz were in the van, sipping sodas and listening to the radio.

"How come Slammer hates you so much?" she asked him.

"Because I'm champion and I beat him all the time. And because of the sponsors. They pay me a lot more. That's why he wants to win so much. He'll earn twice as much money."

"Razz, you didn't really fight him hard. I mean, you just kept pushing him away and ducking his punches. A couple of times you really could have finished him."

Razz tipped up his drink, slurping down the last drops. Then he tucked it into the little bag hanging from the dash.

"I don't like fighting, Allie. It doesn't solve anything."

"Anyway, thanks," she said to him.

"No probs, Brainy. Now, let's check the gear. We gotta roll tonight."

"Where to?" she asked.

"Back home. My sponsor wants to set up a TV interview on the cable station in Barrie. And get this—they want me and Slammer on the same program! What a drag. Now we gotta backtrack."

*Backtrack?* Allie didn't like this news one bit. She didn't know what she wanted anymore. But she wasn't ready to face her parents yet—she knew that much. The last thing she wanted was to go back home.

"No, Razz, I can't go back!" she said.

"Relax, Brainy. We'll go back. You can wait in the van while I do the taping, and we'll be out of there in a couple of hours. We'll leave now, stop along the

way and get some sleep, and be there in
lots of time for me to clean up."

"But—"

"We gotta go," Razz cut in.

"Okay, okay," she said angrily. *What
choice do I have?* she thought.

# Chapter Five

Razz drove for a couple of hours, dipping red twisters into the peanut butter jar before he chomped on them. The night was dark and rainy, with high winds that shook the van.

Allie sat with her feet up on the dash and tried to listen to the music. Her mind was a mess. She was mad at Razz for heading back home, and she was thinking about her parents a lot. And she was worried about the four red circles—especially the one on her calendar. She was still overdue.

Every once in awhile Razz would tell an elephant joke. "Hey, Brainy! How many elephants can you get into a compact car?"

"Who *cares*, Razz?"

"I thought you were Alison the A student. Come on, how many?"

"I don't know."

"Four—two in the front and two in the back!" Razz would laugh like a crazy man.

Allie would groan, but laugh anyway. Sometimes Razz could act pretty strange, but he had always been able to kid her out of a bad mood.

Finally, Razz pulled off the highway onto a gravel side road and parked the van. "Time to catch a few winks, Brainy. I'm whacked. This has been one long day."

Razz pushed a button and his window rolled down. Rain blew into the van.

"Guess I'll have to sleep in here tonight, okay?" The window rolled up, shutting out the rain.

"No probs, Razz. I'll curl up in this seat."

"No, you take the mattress."

"I don't *want* the mattress!" she snapped. *What's wrong with me?* she thought. *I'm starting to sound like my mother.*

"Okay, Brainy. Whatever."

Allie knew that some of her friends wouldn't have stayed up front while Razz slept alone on the mattress. But no way was she moving. She'd had enough of that stuff to last a long time.

Razz set the alarm on the dash clock and climbed in back. He tossed Allie's sleeping bag up to her and turned out the lights. Allie adjusted the bucket seat and tried to get comfortable.

For a long time she couldn't sleep. She stared at the soft blue clock light and listened to the rain beat against the windows and drum on the roof. She had the strangest feeling that something was wrong at home. She was worried about her parents. *They must be sick with worry too*, she thought. *They must be wondering where I am.*

*Should I go back? What would that solve if I did? Nothing, that's what. And what happens if I really am pregnant? I* couldn't *go home then.*

Allie had been pushing that thought away all day. With the excitement of the skateboard competition and the problem with Slammer it had been easy not to think of—that. But now the thought pushed into her mind, and it made her afraid.

It took her a long time to get to sleep.

In the morning the storm was worse. Thunderclaps slammed the dark sky above them as Razz struggled to hold the van steady in the high wind. The lightning was wicked. The wipers flapped like crazy and still it seemed like the van was driving underwater.

After an hour, Allie's thoughts were interrupted by Razz.

"What the—?" he exclaimed.

Allie stared ahead into the rain. Off to the right, she saw red lights flashing. Razz slowed the van and crept toward the lights.

"It's a pickup, with its nose in the ditch," he said. Then he pulled the van onto the shoulder of the highway. They could see a white truck, with a black stripe along the side from headlights to tailgate.

"Hey, that's Slammer's rig," Razz said.

He rammed the shift into Park and opened the door. Rain blew in as he climbed down, slamming the door behind him.

A few minutes later, two shapes floated out of the rain and came toward the van. They disappeared and the back doors opened. A suitcase was tossed in. Razz and Slammer climbed in and Razz crawled forward into the driver's seat. His clothes were soaked. Slammer looked awful. He was drenched, and his white hair was plastered to his head.

*A drowned rat,* thought Allie. *That's what he looks like.*

Slammer looked up at her and grinned. Then he blew her a kiss. She remembered what Razz had said about fighting, so instead of giving him the finger, she smiled as hard as she could. Then she turned around just as Razz pulled the van onto the highway.

"What did you pick *him* up for?" she demanded.

"What could I do, Brainy? He went off the road in the dark and smashed his rad."

"You could have left him there," she answered.

"But we gotta do that stupid TV show."

"Come on back here, Sweet Marie," Slammer sneered. "This mattress is real soft."

Allie stared straight ahead. "Take a hike, loser," she mumbled.

"Hey, gimme a break, you two," Razz snapped. "It's hard enough driving without a fight in the van!"

Finally they were on the 400 again, heading north. The traffic was moving slowly because of the heavy rain. Allie tried to get a weather report on the radio, but all she heard was static. The lightning was too close.

When they got near Barrie, the rain stopped but the wind was worse. Razz was having a hard time holding the van on the road. Allie could see the muscles of his arms bulging as he fought the wheel.

"Hey, Brainy. How many elephants does it take to drive a van through a hurricane?"

By the time they reached the ramp to Essa Road, Razz was creeping along, far below the speed limit. He turned off the highway onto the exit ramp.

Allie peered through the windshield. Past the Holiday Inn, over the hill, was her house. *Wonder if they found my note yet*, she thought.

Razz stopped the van on the gravel shoulder. Then the engine died.

"Hey, look!" he exclaimed.

Slammer scrambled forward and knelt behind the engine cover. "Looks *bad*," he said, his voice shaky.

Ahead of them, to the northwest, the sky was weird. It was a dark purple-gray with a sickening yellow streak across it. The sky was quickly getting darker as the yellow faded. Soon, it was like dusk—but it was only ten o'clock in the morning.

"Look!" Razz said, and pointed to a black cloud up the highway. It seemed to be moving. It wobbled and shifted. Then Allie could see what looked like a crooked black finger coming out of the cloud and reaching down toward the ground.

The cloud *was* moving! It grew larger and larger. The roaring wind was punching the van like giant fists. Dirt from the shoulder of the exit ramp swirled into the air.

"Look," Allie said. "Are those birds flying around in that black cloud?"

"I don't—oh, no, no!"

"Razz! What's the matter?"

"Those aren't birds, they're—they're *boards* or something!"

The black finger was moving through the fields beside the highway, coming right towards them. Allie squinted, trying to figure out what she was seeing.

Then she knew.

In the black cloud, just above the finger, she saw boards and trees and huge, twisted sheets of metal spinning! The finger moved along the edge of the highway, sucking up dirt and gravel and spewing it into the air. It came to a car stopped on the shoulder. Dirt and stones swirled around the car as the whirlwind touched it. The car almost disappeared from sight.

Allie didn't believe what she saw next. The car flipped into the air and landed on its roof, like a toy.

"Razz!" she screamed. "It's coming toward us! Get going! Drive!"

Razz frantically twisted the key. The engine wheezed and groaned and died again.

"Come *on,* man!" Slammer yelled.

"Too late, Allie! Get down!" Razz cried.

But she couldn't. She stared, bug-eyed, out the windshield as the whirlwind came on. It swallowed the main building of the racetrack across the highway from them. The building just seemed to explode. The roof popped up and flew to bits, spinning up into the black cloud. The walls blew outward as if a bomb had gone off inside, and bricks scattered across the track.

The whirlwind came across the highway, flipping two more cars over and sending a tractor-trailer rolling down the bank. Chunks of wood and shingles and pieces of branches began to slam against the van. Something whacked the windshield, cracking it. The fierce wind roared around them.

"We gotta get out of here!" Slammer shouted above the noise. He scrambled to the back of the van and opened the doors. The raging wind thundered into the van.

"Slammer! No!" Razz cried. "Stay inside!"

But it was too late. Slammer was gone. Then he appeared in front of the van, running down the gravel shoulder of the exit ramp. The wind ripped at his clothes, and chunks of wood and other junk spun around him. Then something hit him in the legs and he fell, hard. He rolled, pushed by the wind, and smashed up against a white guardrail post. Through the swirling dust Allie saw him wrap his arms around the post. But the wind plucked him away like a doll. He was picked up and thrown at the van. Slammer's body banged against the windshield, leaving a big red star of blood on the glass before it disappeared.

"Get *down,* Allie!" Razz yelled again.

But she couldn't. She was in a trance. She felt like she was going to vomit as Slammer's blood ran down the windshield. The van rocked in the powerful wind. Then, as the center of the whirlwind came toward the van, it turned and went down Essa Road! The black finger passed through an intersection, scattering cars. It began to climb the hill, ripping trees from the ground and chewing them up. It hit the Holiday Inn. The big picture window blew out and millions of bits of glass climbed into the cloud.

The finger scratched its way up the hill and began blowing the houses on the edge of the hill to pieces. Roofs lifted into the air, spun and fell away. Walls blew out and splintered to bits.

Allie watched the whirlwind disappear over the hill.

Then she began to scream, over and over.

Her parents' house was in that neighborhood.

# Chapter Six

Razz had to shake Allie to get her to stop screaming. He slumped back into his seat, talking as if he was in a daze. "I guess… I guess we should go see if Slammer is… alive…"

Allie squeezed her eyes shut, trying to get her head straight. Was it a nightmare? Had she really seen a tornado snatch Slammer up into the sky and then rip the houses on the hill to bits? When she opened her eyes, the smear of blood on the windshield gave her the answer.

Razz kept trying to start the van. The motor groaned and coughed, but that was all. So they climbed out and walked slowly around to the back of the van. There was no wind now, and the sun seemed to smile from the clear sky as if everything had been a joke. It was dead quiet.

Razz pulled himself up onto the bumper of the van, then to the roof. He peered into the distance, turning slowly as he scanned the fields beside the highway. Slammer was nowhere to be seen. Razz lowered himself to the ground again.

"He's gone," said Razz, his voice quiet. "How could he just disappear?"

Allie shuddered when she thought of it. Slammer's broken body falling out of the whirlwind, landing in a field —or maybe someone's yard.

Then her mind began to wake up. "Razz! Our parents!"

Razz looked at her. "No way, Brainy. My place is miles from here, in the other direction. But—"

Allie felt her heart pounding with fear. "We've got to get to my house, to see if it's...Let's go!"

They began to run down the exit ramp to Essa Road. They soon reached the intersection. There were several overturned cars scattered around. Smoke poured from a pickup truck. A man with his shirt torn to ribbons stood watching it, shaking his head. A few people wandered around as if they were lost. An old man knelt in the middle of the road beside a woman in a pink dress. "Sara," he was saying as he shook her. "Sara, Sara."

"Maybe we should stop and help," Razz suggested.

"No, please," Allie answered. "Let's keep going."

At the corner of Fairview they stopped and looked up the hill at the blasted houses. The most direct route to Allie's house was up the hill and through the yards. But Razz and Allie turned and followed the road. They turned left onto Little Avenue, stepping over huge branches and chunks of debris.

When they got to the top of the hill, near their school, it was as if they had stepped into a science-fiction movie. All around them were the remains of smashed houses. Allie could see into living rooms and bedrooms because walls had blown away. Front lawns were strewn with chunks of wood, fallen trees, broken furniture.

In a daze, they walked down Marshall Street. Around them, voices called kids' names that Allie recognized. People wandered around their yards, staring at places where houses once had been.

"Looks like a war zone," whispered Razz. "Like the city was bombed."

At the corner of Allie's street, they saw her neighbor's dog, Scotty, lying in the middle of the road, his bloody tongue hanging out. A chain was hooked to his collar. At the other end of the chain was the front wall of a doghouse. They walked around the dog. Further down the street Allie saw a car lying on its side in the Dillons' garage. But the walls and the roof of the garage weren't there anymore.

They continued down the street. Then Allie stopped. "Oh, no," she moaned. "No, no, no!"

Where her house had been, only part of a sidewall remained. She could see the stove and the fridge, sitting on a bare floor in the kitchen. Everything else was gone. The big maple tree had been ripped out of the ground. It lay across the yard, its leaves stripped off, and its huge roots sticking up.

Allie put her hands over her eyes. She thought she must be going crazy! She felt Razz put his arm around her.

Allie broke free and began to run. She stumbled across her front lawn and climbed up a pile of loose bricks onto the floor of what used to be her house. It was easy to see that her parents weren't there.

"The basement!" Razz exclaimed. "Maybe they hid there!"

Allie ran to the steps that led to the basement and flung aside half a living-room couch. She went down the stairs, stepping over bricks and pieces of board. The basement was empty.

She slowly climbed the stairs into the sunlight.

"Maybe we should look around the yard," Razz said, "in case…"

He hopped off the floor and onto the grass of the backyard. It was strewn with smashed branches and pieces of other people's houses. Allie followed him.

In the distance they heard sirens, lots of them. Razz and Allie searched the small yard and found nothing. Allie sighed with relief.

"Maybe they weren't at home when the tornado hit," she said hopefully. "Yeah, that's right! Today is Monday, so Dad would be at work and Mom would be…"

Her voice trailed off. Her mom would be at home, she knew.

Razz seemed to read her mind. "She could have been out shopping or something, Brainy. I know it's hard, but try not to worry until we know for sure."

He bent over and picked something up. "This yours?" he asked. He handed Allie a small portable radio.

"No."

Allie snapped it on. It was working. She tuned it to the local station.

"Tornado" was the first word she heard. The announcer was in a panic, talking fast about the storm and the damage. So far, four deaths had been reported.

"Residents whose houses have been damaged or destroyed are urged not to try to enter their homes. Emergency centers are being set up in the following places."

One of the places he mentioned was the public school four blocks from Allie's house.

"Let's go," Allie said. "Maybe Mom and Dad are there."

"Okay, Brainy, let's go."

They walked around the house and back toward the street. At the corner of the front yard, Allie saw a piece of white paper caught in the stripped branches of the hedge. She thought of the note she had left for her mom and dad. She remembered the four red circles. She remembered writing "You'll be better off without me."

Allie began to cry.

# Chapter Seven

Razz and Allie hurried down the street toward the school where the emergency center was set up.

Allie whacked her fist against the side of her leg as she walked. *I never should have run away*, she thought. *What did it solve? Nothing, that's what. Now the four red circles don't seem to be so important. Not even the one on the calendar.*

Allie looked once more at the smashed houses all along the street. The piles of brick and boards once were houses where her neighbors used to live. *Nothing could be as bad as this*, she thought.

Razz kicked a big batt of pink fiberglass insulation out of their way. The stuff was littered all over the streets and lawns. He looked at Allie.

"Come on, Brainy, don't cry. Everything will be all right. You'll see. Just hang in there until we get to the school, okay? I'm sure we'll find them and they'll be safe."

"I hope so, Razz," she said, wiping the tears away with the back of her hand. The sound of his voice calmed her a little.

They were turning the corner onto St. John Street when they heard someone shout. "Her! Her! Look, she could do it!"

Razz and Allie stopped. There were five people standing beside the foundation of a house. The house was gone, but there was a huge jumble of boards and smashed furniture piled there, like giant matchsticks. As Allie looked at the pile, the first thing she thought was *Pick-up Sticks*. It was a game she used to play when she was a little kid.

A tall, thin man rushed up to them. "Please help us!" he shouted, grabbing Allie by the arm. "Our baby...you've got to help."

He wrenched Allie's arm, and she pulled away, frightened.

"Hey, take it easy, man," said Razz.

The man tried to grab Allie again. She saw terror in his twisted face and shrank back.

"Please!" he cried again. "You've got to help."

Another man had joined them. He spoke more calmly. "My friend's baby is trapped in the cellar of his house," he explained, pointing to where the three people stood looking under the pile of lumber that used to be a house. "We've got to get her out before all that junk collapses. If that happens, the baby will be—"

He looked at his friend, then back to Allie and Razz. "Will you help?"

"Why don't you do it?" Razz asked. "There are three men, counting you two."

"Because there's no way in except a little opening." He took Razz's arm and led him toward the others as he spoke. Allie and the father followed. "None of us can fit into it," he went on.

A short, plump woman was crying hysterically, moaning, "My baby, my baby," again and again. Her dress was ripped and tears made white streaks in the dirt on her face. She stared into the mass of jumbled lumber. Allie could hear a baby wailing from somewhere in the mess.

The father pointed to the cellar window. Allie looked in and she could see right away what the man meant. There was a small opening there. A person her size could probably squeeze through the gap and get into the basement.

"Maybe it would be better to wait until the fire department or someone with equipment could get here," Razz said.

"Are you kidding?" the father answered, his voice angry. "Have you seen the streets? They're clogged with trees and hunks of houses. It'll be hours before anyone can get through."

Just as he spoke, the huge mass of twisted and jumbled lumber shifted, groaning and creaking as it settled. The mother shrieked and cried even louder.

"John, do something! She'll die in there!"

Allie didn't know what to do. She peered in through the window, then scanned the faces of the people.

"Don't do it, Brainy," warned Razz. "You'll never get out again."

Allie was scared. *Razz is right*, she thought.

She said, "I don't think—"

"Oh, no," said one of the other men. "Look!"

From the front corner of the house, a wisp of black smoke curled up into the still air.

The mother shrieked again. The other woman and man began talking at the same time. The father looked over at the smoke.

"The fireplace! I had a fire on in the family room when the tornado hit. It must be spreading!"

Allie was on her knees at the cellar window before she knew what she was doing.

"Brainy, no!" Razz yelled.

Allie didn't see the father shove Razz roughly out of the way. She felt someone grab her ankles.

"I'll lower you down," said the other man. "Gently now."

He let her slide slowly into the basement until her hands touched the carpeted floor.

"Okay, let go," she said over her shoulder.

Allie fell into a heap. She got onto her hands and knees and looked around. It was dark and gloomy. The basement ceiling had caved in, leaving only a narrow crawl space around the outer walls of the house. Allie couldn't see the baby's crib in the far corner, but she could hear the crying. As she started to crawl along the wall, a wisp of smoke floated toward her.

She reached the far wall of the house easily, scraping her back on the broken boards a few times. She turned left and headed for the corner where the crib was. When she got there, she knew things were going to be tough. When the ceiling had collapsed, it had pinned the crib against the wall. Now the crib was trapped in a cage of broken lumber.

The baby wore a white cloth diaper and a tiny white T-shirt with pink elephants on it. She was blonde, with curly hair. She was crying softly.

Allie couldn't see a way to lift her out. Gently she pulled at the wooden bars of the crib. The boards above groaned and shifted. *I can't lower the side*, she thought, *or the whole mess will fall in on us.*

Allie stopped to think. She was surprised at how calm she felt. Crawling along the wall, she had been terrified. She was still scared, but now she could think clearly. She smelled smoke again— stronger this time. *I'd better do something soon*, she thought.

Allie then noticed that the mattress rested on a frame with springs, and the frame was hung onto the crib with hooks. The hooks fit onto metal prongs attached to the crib, so that the mattress could be raised or lowered.

Taking a deep breath, Allie decided what to do. She slid under the crib and reached up to unhook the bedspring at one corner. The mattress was heavy. She had to heave upwards with all her strength and slip the hook off the prong. It worked. The mattress sagged suddenly at one corner, startling the baby. *Poor little kid*, thought Allie as the baby began to wail louder. Allie slid to the other corner, heaved up with all her might and unhooked the bedspring, which then dropped on top of her.

Carefully, she worked her way out from under the heavy mattress. The squalling baby began to slide toward the floor and Allie easily reached over and pulled her out.

She held the tiny girl in her arms, softly talking to her. The baby grew quiet. *How am I going to carry her out?* thought Allie. *I can't crawl holding her.* She looked around and found an answer.

Taking a blanket from the crib, she folded it several times to make it soft, lay the baby on it and began to crawl backward, gently pulling the baby along behind her. As she dragged, the baby began to giggle and kick her feet.

Allie got to the corner of the basement just as the pile of lumber shrieked and groaned. She snatched up the baby and held it to her as the floor collapsed further with a rumble and crash, sending clouds of dust over them. Allie moaned. She was sure she was going to die.

Outside, she could hear voices yelling. Razz's voice was loudest. "Allie! Allie!" he shouted. She could hear the fear in his voice.

"I'm okay," she yelled. She began to crawl again, very slowly, dragging the baby girl, inching backward on her hands and knees.

She felt something stab into her back. Behind her, the boards had collapsed to within a foot of the carpet, and a long spike projected down. She lay the baby down again and lowered herself to her stomach. Inching backward, she slid carefully under the nail. But she couldn't get flat enough. The nail dug into her, scoring a sharp, painful line along her back and catching on her bra strap. She struggled and felt the nail let go, then inched backward again. Then she stopped and carefully dragged the baby under the nail.

The smoke was really bad now. Allie and the baby began to cough.

"There she is!" the father shouted. "Come on, kid, you're almost home."

Allie tried to move more quickly. The baby was coughing and wailing, her nose running. She was twisting and struggling to get away from the smoke.

Finally, Allie was below the window. She got to her knees and pulled the baby to her. Lifting the little girl into her arms, Allie wrapped her in the blanket, covering her head. The baby screamed in protest.

"Just a little longer," Allie crooned to her. She turned and lifted the baby up to the waiting arms that stuck through the opening at the window, just as the black smoke boiled around her.

Allie couldn't see. The smoke choked her and she began to cough and retch. Her lungs burned and she felt as if the air was being squeezed out of her. She could hear the fire now, crackling and roaring. Trying to stand, she bashed her head on a board and fell down again. She got to her knees, fighting for breath, and slid her hands up the cement wall, feeling for the opening. Then strong hands grabbed hers and began to pull. The boards around her groaned and collapsed with a cracking roar as Allie was dragged upward.

She was out. She lay on the grass in the sunlight, gasping.

Allie struggled and sat up, trying to get her breath. Around her, voices cried and rattled. But this time the voices were relieved and happy.

"You okay, Brainy?" Razz's voice sounded wonderful.

"Yeah," Allie gasped. "I think so."

Razz helped Allie to her feet. The adults surrounded her, touching her, telling her how brave she was. Allie didn't feel brave—just embarrassed and sore. The mother, holding the baby tightly, thanked Allie again and again, talking through her tears. They made Allie tell them her name. And that made Allie remember her own family.

She said to Razz, "Let's get going."

# Chapter Eight

Allie and Razz were back on the street, hurrying to the school. The air was warm and the sun shone brightly.

They had to keep going around things or stepping over things. A crushed baby carriage, tree limbs, a TV set, smashed couches. Allie was terrified that she would see a dead body in the road.

Sirens screamed in the distance. People yelled constantly. They shouted names and called out orders to each other.

Finally Allie and Razz reached the elementary school that was serving as an emergency shelter. Many of the windows had been blown out, but Allie could tell that the whirlwind had not hit directly. Some of the houses around it were still okay. They had no windows now, and some had a lot of shingles missing, but they were all right compared to Allie's house.

Allie and Razz went in the front door of the school, their feet grinding on broken glass. People were moving back and forth quickly through the dark hall. There were cops, firemen and people in other uniforms. But these people weren't like the ones on the street. They all seemed to have a purpose.

Allie and Razz went to the main office. A fat woman in a cop uniform was talking quickly into a walkie-talkie. The cigarette in the corner of her mouth bounced up and down as she talked. When she said, "Over!" Allie told her she wanted to find her parents.

"What's your name?" the woman asked.

Allie told her. The woman looked at a clipboard that had a lot of dog-eared sheets of paper clipped to it.

"I have nobody of that name working here," she said. "But we've only been set up for ten minutes, so we might hear something. We've just started to make up a lost-and-found list. So if your parents are looking for you, I can tell them you're okay."

The walkie-talkie crackled. The woman held it to her ear for a minute, then the cigarette began to bounce again. "Okay, make sure the gas, electricity and water are turned off for the entire area. We already have two gas fires reported.

We got one clear route to the hospital, along Elm, then west on Ranch Avenue. When does the army get here?"

The walkie-talkie crackled some more, then the woman said, "Over."

Razz asked, "Are you calling in the army?"

"Yeah," the woman answered, "the base is pretty close and we need lots of manpower to close the area off, search for injured people, prevent looters— all that."

"Looters?" Allie replied. "What kind of creep would do that?"

"You'd be surprised," was all she said.

People ran in and out of the office, firing questions at the woman or giving her reports. She was the only calm person in the school, it seemed.

When the office was empty of people again, she said to Allie, "Was your house damaged?"

"It's gone!" Allie replied. She began to cry again. She felt Razz's arm around her.

"Do you know where the gym is?"

"Yes."

"Go there. We're putting up a huge poster on the wall. Soon as we get information on people—where they are and how they are—we'll post it. Now, you live nearby, right?"

Allie said yes again.

"Okay, then you can be a big help because you know some of the people around here. We're going to need lots of help in the next couple of days, Allie. Lots of it. Will you help us?"

"Of course," Allie said.

"Good. Now, off you go. And," the woman added as the walkie-talkie crackled at her, "try not to worry. Your parents are likely okay. It just may take a while to find that out."

Allie turned to go but Razz stayed put. He told the woman about Slammer.

She shook her head and made a note on her clipboard.

"Was he a friend of yours?"

Razz looked at Allie. "Sort of," he answered. "We don't know his real name."

"All right, we'll keep an eye out for his...for him."

Razz nodded. "Um, do you need anyone to do some driving?" he asked.

The woman looked up from the clipboard. She lit another cigarette from the butt of the last one. "Well, probably we'll need that, yeah."

"I've got a van. Maybe I can help," he said.

"Sure. Is it here?"

"No, but I think I can get it here in a little while."

"Great. Come on back in when you can."

Razz turned to Allie. "Will you be okay, Brainy?"

"Sure, Razz."

When they were out in the dark, busy hall, Razz added, "I'd...I don't know...I'd sort of feel better if I could do something, you know? Like you did back there at the house."

Allie went to the gym. There were about twenty people there, setting up tables, talking into walkie-talkies, spreading mats on the floor. She saw grouchy old Mr. Beekman, who had chased her out of his backyard a million times when she was little. He was wrapping a bandage on Mrs. Pearce's arm. She lived two doors from Allie and right now she looked a little rough.

Allie went over to a guy in a fireman's uniform.

"Can I help?" she asked.

"You know how to use one of these?" he asked, holding up a walkie-talkie.

"No."

The fireman showed her.

"We're working on a list of missing persons," he said. "Any news you get from the other end," he held up the walkie-talkie, "you make note of it. Mostly, you'll be putting names on this list, but after awhile, you'll get news, from the hospital, from the streets, that someone has been found. You put them on this list. Got it?"

"Got it," Allie said.

"Someone will collect your sheets and put the dope on the big posters over there." He pointed to the wall across the gym from Allie. One huge poster was headed MISSING, the other, FOUND.

Allie sat down behind the table and pulled the stack of sheets toward her. On the top of the first sheet she wrote the names of her parents.

# Chapter Nine

Allie sat behind the table for the rest of the day. She was very busy. She got calls from the hospital, the police station, the radio station, and from the streets. The list on the big poster headed MISSING grew and grew, and they had to start another one. Her parents' names were still on the top of the list.

No matter how busy she was, she couldn't stop thinking about her parents. Her imagination ran wild at times. She pictured them crushed by a fallen wall or sucked up into the black finger-cloud like Slammer. When those thoughts grabbed hold of her mind, she got scared and cried again.

But she was still able to do something useful. It didn't take Allie long to get used to talking into the walkie-talkie. It reminded her of all the war movies and cop movies she had seen. She got to recognize the voices on the other end. The hospital voice was a woman. The voice from her neighborhood was a guy. She could tell he wasn't very old. He sounded a little like one of the guys at the skateboarding meet who had wanted Razz to autograph his new skateboard.

After it got dark, Allie had to work with a big flashlight. The gym was lit with big gas camping lanterns. It was a little creepy.

Later, Allie asked someone to take over while she went to the washroom. It was dark in the halls of the school too, and lanterns lighted them. It was eerie. Shadows moved along the walls and groans came out of the darkness. The halls were full of people. Some lay on mats, some sat against the wall, in a daze. A lot of them were injured, waiting for rides to the hospital. Some were getting fixed up by the dozens of nurses and St. John Ambulance workers. Kids cried.

She took a walk past the office. The same woman was there in the same place, talking into the walkie-talkie. She looked very tired. The hall by the office seemed full of uniformed men and women—cops, army, gas company, electric company, medics. It was like everyone in town was gathered in this one building.

A few hours later, the lights came on in the gym and Allie snapped off the flashlight she had been using. She was taking down a name on the FOUND list when she looked up and saw Razz standing in front of the table.

He looked awful. His yellow silk T-shirt was torn and bloody. He had scrapes all over his arms. His face was dirty and tired looking. But he was smiling.

"Hey, Brainy, looks like you're an important person around here."

"Not me. I just answer the radio."

Razz tossed a chunk of chocolate cake wrapped in plastic to her. "Hungry?"

"Yeah, thanks." Allie unwrapped the package and bit into the cake. It tasted wonderful.

"Sorry I took so long," Razz went on. He fished a couple of red twisters out of his pocket and began to munch. "I've been hauling passengers to the hospital.

83

The ones who aren't too badly hurt. They sent me over here to pick up a load, so I thought I'd come and see how you're doing. I guess you haven't heard."

"Heard what?" Allie was too tired to fill in the blanks.

"Your parents are at the hospital."

"Really? Are they okay?"

"Well, your mom got pretty banged up. Nothing real serious, though. Your dad is fine. He was at work when the tornado hit—and your mom was shopping. She was hurt when the mall got hit. I saw them. I told them you were okay."

Allie said nothing for a minute.

"Razz," she said at last, "can you take me over there?"

"Sure, Brainy. No probs. Let's go."

"Wait a second. I gotta find someone to replace me first."

Before she left the table, Allie wrote her parents' names on the FOUND list.

# Chapter Ten

The hospital was a madhouse. The emergency ward, the halls, the rooms were packed with beds and cots and worried people. Nurses slipped back and forth quickly through the noisy halls. Every few seconds a doctor's name was called over a loudspeaker.

Razz led Allie to a big ward on the second floor. "I'll leave you here, Brainy," he said. "Gotta get back to work. Will you be okay?"

"Yeah, no probs, Razz. See you later."

*I wish I felt as brave as I sound,* Allie thought. She wanted to go back with Razz. She didn't want to see the Hurt Look her father would give her and the I Told You So Look that would come to her mother's face as soon as Allie walked in. But she knew she had to stay.

She took a breath and walked into the crowded ward.

She saw her mother at the far end of the room, propped up on a bed. One leg was in a thick white cast that was attached to a rack over the bed. One of her arms was in a cast too. Allie's father stood beside the bed.

"Hi, Mom. Hi, Dad," she said as she got to the bed.

Allie's father spun around. He grabbed her and held her tighter than he had ever done. He said nothing. He held her for a long time.

"Allie!" her mother cried, her voice starting to wind up. "Where have you been? If I could get out of this bed I'd give you a darn good slap!" Then she calmed down and asked, "Are you all right?"

"Sure, Mom. I'm fine. What about you?"

"Oh, I'm all right, now. Where were you? We were worried sick. We even called the police."

Allie looked at her mother. Her mother's blonde hair was a mess. She had a purple bruise around her left eye. She looked like she'd been through a war. Allie's father didn't look so hot either. His suit was dirty and wrinkled and there was an angry red scratch across his forehead.

"I left you a note, Mom. I ran away."

"What on earth *for?*" her mother almost shrieked.

"Maybe we should talk about this some other time," her father said. "This isn't the right—"

"*No*! You're always avoiding things," her mother cut in angrily.

"I *don't* always avoid things! You're the one—"

Allie clapped her hands over her ears and shut her eyes.

"*Stop*! Stop arguing!" she shouted.

She opened her eyes again. Her father looked embarrassed. Her mother hung her head and picked at the bandage on her leg.

"Allie, what was it?" she asked softly.

Allie looked into her mother's bruised face, then at her father. She thought about why she had run away—the fighting between her parents, the four red circles. Three on her report card. One on her calendar.

*Should I tell them?* she thought. *How much should I tell them? Will it do any good?*

Then Allie realized they were going to find out anyway. She took a deep breath and started talking.

She told them everything—about the three subjects she failed, about Jack and how she might be pregnant, about the skateboard meet and about Slammer's death in the whirlwind. When she was finished, she was crying. And she felt worthless.

Allie's mother and father were silent for a minute. They looked shocked. But they didn't yell at her.

Her mother said, "Are you sure?"

Allie knew what she meant. "Yeah, pretty sure, Mom. I'm way overdue."

Allie's father ran his fingers through his thin hair. "I guess we shouldn't think of you as our little girl anymore," he said quietly. "You've been through a lot. Are you and Jack—"

"Dad, I'm through with him," she cut in. "I don't even want him to know. He's not important anymore."

He gave her a strange look. "No, I guess he isn't," he agreed.

Allie's mother said, "Come here, Allie."

Allie stepped closer to the bed, half expecting the shrieks to start. But her mother took her hand and held it. Her face looked serious and worried.

"You forgot to tell us a few things, didn't you, dear?"

*What did she mean*, Allie thought. "Honest, Mom, I've told you everything. Honest."

"You didn't tell us you saved that baby's life. You didn't tell us how you helped out at the school. Razz told us all about it."

"Mom, that doesn't mean anything," said Allie.

"Of course it means something," her mother said. "It means a lot. We're proud of you, Allie. You're a very brave kid. And you're a very *good* kid."

Allie looked at her father. He was smiling. He pointed to the window.

"Look," was all he said.

Allie let go of her mother's hand and stepped over to the window beside the bed. She looked out across the sunny neighborhood. She could see the scar-like path the tornado had left as it chewed up trees and smashed houses. It changed people's lives forever. She remembered what Razz had said, that it looked as if the neighborhood had been bombed.

Then she began to pay attention to the small groups of people. Already they were cleaning up the streets, moving furniture out of houses to waiting trucks, starting over. In the distance she saw a tiny figure on a roof, swinging a hammer.

Her father's voice came from behind her. "I guess we—the three of us— I guess we've got some things to work out. We've got some rebuilding to do."

Allie turned to see he was looking at her mother.

Her mother nodded. "Yes," she whispered. "Yes, you're right."

"Mom, Dad, we can do it together, can't we?"

Allie's mother and father spoke at the same time, "We can try."

## Author's Note

There are lots of words to describe the atmosphere on that final day of May—brooding, ominous, foreboding— but I'd choose *weird*. The day before, Thursday, had been stormy, with thunder and downpours and damaging winds. Friday dawned hot and humid and stayed that way. When I walked through Innisdale Secondary School's parking lot at 4:30 PM, the air was heavy and clammy. The sky was dark gray, the clouds low. On the towering maples in front of the school, not a leaf stirred. The birds were strangely silent.

When I drove down the hill on Fairview Avenue it had grown so dark it was like nighttime. In the northwest, the sky was an ugly purple with a yellow tinge, like a bruise. I turned onto Highway 400 and headed north, passing through a few showers on my way home. I put a rock 'n' roll tape on the deck to brighten the mood.

When I got home, I turned on the radio to hear the news. Two words struck me: Barrie Tornado. I had missed being swept up in the whirlwind by twenty-five minutes. On that afternoon, fourteen tornadoes ripped through southern Ontario, killing twelve people, injuring dozens of others and causing about $100 million in property damage. The largest tornado left a path of destruction 90 kilometers long—much greater than the average. The Barrie Tornado was really five separate tornadoes that slammed into the town at 5:00 PM, May 31, 1985.

This novel is based on the tornado and its aftermath. With many other teachers, I was part of the clean-up crews that set to work immediately to bring order back to the community. Thousands of people helped. *Death Wind* is dedicated to them, and to the many who suffered from the storm.

—*William Bell*

William Bell is an award-winning author of more than a dozen books for young adults. Born in Toronto, Ontario, in 1945, he has been a high school English teacher and department head, and an instructor at the Harbin University of Science and Technology, the Foreign Affairs College in Beijing and the University of British Columbia. He lives in Ontario.

The following is an excerpt from
another exciting Orca Soundings novel,
*Riley Park* by Diane Tullson.

# Chapter One

In the Safeway parking lot, I drop two flats of beer into the back of my car. I leave the hatch open and wait for Darius to arrive with the hotdog stuff. I notice a girl getting off the bus across the parking lot at the bus stop. I'd recognize her from a mile away: Rubee.

Rubee is wearing her Safeway shirt and she's walking fast, like maybe she's late for work. Her dark hair is loose on her shoulders.

Darius shows up and slings the grocery bags into the car, fitting them around the beer and my hockey bag.

As Rubee walks, she combs her hair back with her fingers and catches it into a thick ponytail.

Darius says, "She is so hot."

Darius is watching her too.

I say, "Hot, yes. But Rubee is beautiful."

Rubee is a senior like Darius and me, but she goes to a different school. I've never seen Rubee anywhere but here, at Safeway. We always choose Rubee's checkout line, even if hers is twice as long as the others. Rubee is worth the wait.

Darius says, "Weird that she took the bus. Her boyfriend always drops her off."

I've never seen her boyfriend, but Rubee wears a guy's ring on her thumb.

Plus, a couple of months ago, she rejected Darius when he asked her out. Go figure—he asked her if she'd like to spend the night with a wild man.

I say, "You've seen Rubee's boyfriend?"

Darius nods. "He has a nice car."

I glance at my Civic. One fender is a different color and the left taillight is covered with a red plastic bag.

I say, "Maybe it's her brother."

"No." Darius turns to me. "It was her boyfriend. But she took the bus today, so that means he isn't her boyfriend anymore."

"Maybe he had to work or something."

Darius says, "From the car he drives, he makes way more money than a regular job."

"You think he sells drugs or something?" I watch as Rubee enters the Safeway. "She wouldn't go out with a guy like that."

Darius looks at me. "And you would know?"

"Yes. She's too sweet."

He says, "Sweet girls fall the hardest."

I say, "How can you be sure they broke up?"

"Let's just run with it," Darius says. "You think she's too sweet for you?"

My face grows hot. "No."

"So go ask her out."

"No."

He laughs again, and I'm getting pissed off.

I say, "Not today. I'll ask her out sometime when I'm wearing my team jacket. A hockey jacket makes a busted nose look tough." Instead of ugly. "And I'll wear my ring, my junior hockey championship ring."

Darius says, "If you don't ask her out right now, I will."

My hands curl into fists. "Like she'd go out with you, Wildman."

He shrugs. "Only one way to find out." He slams down the hatch on my car and strides toward the store.

I catch up with him. "We've got everything we need. Let's go."

But he's in the store and in Rubee's line.

Ahead of us, an old woman in sweatpants smacks coins onto the counter. She is ranting to Rubee about an expired coupon. She doesn't have much on the conveyor: bananas, toilet paper—the cheap stuff—and some liquid meal replacement old people drink. The cans of meal replacement have a red clearance sticker. They must be close to the best-before date. Maybe they've expired.

Rubee speaks quietly to the woman as she pushes several coins back to her.

The woman grins, gathers the coins, grabs her bag of groceries and scuttles out of the store. The guy in front of us shovels the rest of his stuff onto the conveyor. Rubee counts the old woman's coins into the cash drawer. She looks up and sees me. She smiles.

I look at her hand. She's not wearing the ring.

I watch her scan the guy's groceries. She's wearing a black cord bracelet with a round red stone. The stone slides back and forth on her wrist as she works. But she's not wearing the ring. She smiled at me, she's not wearing the ring and we're standing in her line with nothing to buy.

I grab a pack of gum and toss it in a shopping basket.

Darius laughs. "Corbin, if you're asking her out, you'll need more time than it takes to ring in one pack of gum." He turns and snags a half-filled cart someone has left unattended. He pushes the cart into Rubee's line.

I say to him, "I'm not asking her out. I'm not ready. If she says no, I'll lose my once-in-a-lifetime chance." I peer into the cart. "Nice. You were right out of Huggies."

Behind us, a woman says, "Now where did I leave my cart?"

Darius says, "Once in a lifetime? You're asking her out, not proposing."

I pull a package out of the pile of groceries in the cart. "And animal crackers."

The woman's voice is louder now. "I swear, I left my cart right here."

Rubee looks up then, sees the woman. She glances at our cart and rolls her eyes. She picks up the security phone.

Darius says, "Oops, I seem to have someone else's cart." And he leaves it there. Just abandons the cart in the line.

He walks by me and past the guy ahead of us until he's standing in front of Rubee. Rubee puts the phone down.

I elbow my way past the guy so that I'm beside Darius. I struggle to meet her eyes. "Uh, sorry about the, uh, cart."

Darius just stands there. Finally he says to me, "Anything else?"

I glance at Rubee. She looks like she's waiting for me to say something. Her eyes have little gold flecks. I feel my cheeks turn bright red. I hand her the pack of gum.

She smiles. "Just the gum? No diapers?"

I shake my head and hand her the money.

Darius sighs. He says to me, "Are you done?"

I look at my shoes.

"I'll take that as a yes." He turns to Rubee. "Riley Park, tonight. I'm saving myself for you."

She looks at him and crosses her arms. "Unlikely," she says, "on both counts."

"We'll go swimming."

"You might, but you'll freeze."

"I'm a wild man." Darius smiles at her. "I'll bring blankets."

It's not like Darius is super attractive. He's built, but he's not that tall. He spends a fortune on his hair. Maybe that's why the girls go for him. Darius reaches into a pail of plastic-wrapped flower bouquets by the check stand. He selects an arrangement of red and white roses. Water from the bouquet drips on the counter. He presents the flowers to Rubee. "These are for you," he says. "A token of my love."

Rubee takes the flowers and smiles.

Darius says, "Riley Park. Tonight. Nothing complicated, Rubee. You're your own woman. No one telling you what to do—you're in control. Come to the party if you want, bring some friends, have a few laughs, or don't. It's totally up to you."

The guy with the groceries tells us to piss off and get out of the line.

Darius ignores him. "Later, I hope," Darius says to Rubee, and he blows her a kiss.

The following is an excerpt from
another exciting Orca Soundings novel,
*Running the Risk* by Lesley Choyce.

# Chapter One

The gunmen arrived at Burger Heaven shortly after midnight on Friday. I was on the frontline, taking orders along with Lacey and Cam. It was like a dream at first. The place had been quiet except for some workmen laughing over their French fries, and a couple of slightly drunk kids from school goofing around at a table by the windows.

And then the door opened and two guys with ski masks on walked in nervously. One walked straight to me. The other went to Lacey. As they approached, the guns came up. Lacey, Cam and I froze. The room suddenly went dead quiet except for the sound of hamburgers sizzling in the back and the buzz of the overhead fluorescent lights. I'd never even noticed the hum of the fluorescent lights before.

The guy with the gun pointed at Lacey spoke first. "Open it, girl."

Lacey froze.

"I said open it."

The guy with the gun on me said nothing. I was looking at Lacey. And then at Cam. There was a panic button on the floor beneath each register. A silent alarm. You triggered it and the cops would know we were in trouble. I saw Cam looking down at the floor.

But something told me that right here, right now, hitting that button would be the wrong thing to do. These two guys were nervous. I was looking my gunman right in the eyes. I knew there was something there. These guys were whacked on something. Anything could make them freak. The guns were real. Everything was real.

And that's when it kicked in.

This feeling of calm.

"Be cool," I said to the guy pointing the gun at Lacey. Then I looked at the guy with the gun on me. I stared straight into his eyes, and then I looked at the barrel of the gun like it was no big deal.

"I'm going to push this key and the drawer will open," I said. "Okay?"

My gunman nodded. I pushed the key, and the drawer opened. I saw one of the workmen get up. At first I thought he was going to try to do something. And I didn't want that.

But I was wrong. First he and then his buddy got up and slipped out the front door. Lacey's gunman turned and aimed in their direction. He pulled the trigger and the shot was deafening. "Shit," was all he said. The bullet must have hit the ceiling because no glass shattered. He turned back quickly and pushed the gun into Lacey's face.

"Here," I said, cleaning all the bills out of my register and handing them across the counter. "Now I'll get you the rest," I said.

"Yeah," my gunman said.

I walked to Lacey and made sure it was obvious what I was doing. I hit the key, the drawer opened and I offered over more bills.

Then I walked over to Cam's station and did the same. It was only money.

Nothing to die for, that's for sure. It was all clear as day in my head.

The two gunmen stuffed the money into their coat pockets, turned and ran. As soon as they were out the door and away from the parking lot, I hit the silent alarm.

Lacey began to cry and Cam said the stupidest thing in the world. "Why'd you give them the money?"

"You all right, Lacey?" I asked.

"No, Sean," she said, "I'm not all right."

"What were you thinking?" Cam asked. Somehow he wasn't getting it.

The kids at the table were standing up now. "I don't freaking believe it," one of them said and then puked on the floor.

Riley and Jeanette, who'd been listening from the food-prep area, came up to the counter now.

"Is everyone all right?" Riley asked.

"Yeah, we're all alive anyway," I said.

"Did you see what this jerk did?" Cam said, pointing at me.

"Yeah," Jeanette said. "I saw what he did. He saved you from getting killed."

Cam looked mad. He looked at me like it was all my fault.

The kids at the table out front were helping their buddy who had just barfed on the floor get himself together. Then they headed for the door. I probably should have asked them to stay until the cops came, but I didn't. I understood they wanted to get the hell out of here. I knew who they were, so I didn't bother to ask them to stay. The police could find them for information if they needed to.

Jeanette was holding Lacey.

Cam was blathering. "This isn't worth it," he said. "I'm quitting this stupid job. Now." He walked around the counter and kicked over a chair. Then he left. I didn't ask him to stay either.

When the police arrived, two officers in bulletproof vests pushed open the glass door and walked in, guns raised. I watched their eyes as they looked at us and then scanned Burger Heaven. I noticed the buzz of the lights again.

"They're gone," I said.

The guns came down and the cops moved forward.

"Anyone hurt?" one of them asked. Two more policemen came in the door.

"No," I said. "I think we're okay."

"Do you know which way they went?"

I shook my head no.

One of the policemen saw the bullet hole in the ceiling. "You guys had a close call," he said. "That wasn't a cap gun."

It was about then that I noticed something about the way I was feeling. My heart was still pumping so loud I could hear it in my ears, and my breathing was a bit ragged.

But the weird part was that I was feeling great. And I'd been feeling this way from the moment the robber put the gun up to my face.

For more information on all the books in
the Orca Soundings series, please visit
www.orcabook.com.